A COLLECTION OF SHORT STORIES

STILL WATERS, DEEP THOUGHTS

The little grey pebble skipped across the surface of the ice cold lake, propelled with whirling velocity by the skilled hand of an 11 year old boy who stood at the very edge of the water, a glassy look in his eyes, staring vacantly toward the silent horizon.

There was not a cloud in the sky and it was bitterly cold. A sudden shudder swept through the boy as though an invisible ghost had somehow passed right through him. He was alone. Utterly alone. Reflecting on the vast emptiness which lay all around him, it struck him that there really was no-one to turn to, no-one to ask for help. What if he starved? What if he had an accident?

Feeling a rising panic in his chest, he shut his eyes tight and clenched his small fists. Summoning the inner strength of mind that he needed to push down all those thoughts of despair and isolation, he took a series of deep breaths.

Gradually and by degrees, he slowly began to return to serenity and gazed once more upon his exquisite surroundings. This was the Canadian wilderness and he was very much in the backcountry. His best guess was that he was situated around 250 kilometers north of Saskatoon. The journey he'd been on just to get here had been something Tom Sawyer might have been proud of.

Fleeing an abusive, alcoholic father who had beaten him every-day since his mother had passed away after a short illness the previous winter had led him to this spot. The boy had decided it was now a matter of sink or swim. He had never been close to his father and things had gotten a lot worse since it had become just the two of them. He had no brother or sister to provide either comfort or relief and without his mother to confide in, the atmosphere in the house had become increasingly toxic. The loss of his closest companion had cut deep into the boy's heart.

There were frequent passing urges to take revenge for the cruelty his father was inflicting upon him. As if the two of them weren't suffering enough trying to cope with the grief of losing the matriarch of the family, his father simply sought refuge in the bottle and progressively became ever more violent and unpredictable.

Ultimately, he couldn't hold it anymore. Matters came to a head one night when having made himself a makeshift dinner of beef hash - his mother's nurturing had equipped him with rudimentary culinary skills - and completed his school homework, the father had returned from a local bar, full of beer, spiteful in expression and malicious in word. Staggering into their little kitchen, it was immediately clear that the father was interested only in igniting an argument and set out to provoke his son by firing a whole host of nasty barbs at his young son, one after another, goading him mercilessly.

"Tyler, you little bastard," leered the insufferable father. "Even your own god-damned mother couldn't stand you. No wonder she's dead. YOU killed her! Anyone having to run around after a deadbeat like you wouldn't stick around for long." He nodded decisively, slurring his words as he went. "I know all about it, you see. You shouldn't even be here! You were nothing more than a god-damned accident."

A perfect storm of volcanic emotion rose up in the boy's chest. All at once, he wanted to throw himself on the floor, sob uncontrollably and seek acceptance from his wayward father. His father, for all his faults, was all he had in this world. There was no-one else. No other living relatives that he knew of. Tyler felt utterly abject.

Despite his feelings of gloomy resignation, there was a far greater emotion welling up inside him, the power of which was uncontrollable. Surging like the waves of a raging tsunami as it hurtles toward landfall, he couldn't have held this greater power down even if he had wanted to.

Now he could feel the bullying figure standing over him as he sat at the table, jabbing his finger into his shoulder repeatedly. The savage torrent of verbal abuse faded into something resembling white noise as young Tyler's consciousness switched imperceptibly into autopilot mode.

He couldn't swear to being fully cognizant of his actions - it seemed to him more the case that somebody else had taken a seat at the controls and was guiding his response mechanisms. You could speculate that the boy had entered fight or flight mode.

In a flash, using his right hand Tyler clutched the knife he had just been using to cut up his beef hash and making a rapid arc with the sharp protruding blade pointed toward his uncompromising assailant, he sliced right through his father's jugular with the grace of a professional tennis player's honed backhand. This unspeakable act of butchery along with the immediate aftermath was shocking to behold.

Somewhere deep in the recesses of his mind, an invisible demon pressed the button on a stopwatch. The last ten seconds of his father's life ticked away in front of him. It was a macabre scene. What he was witnessing no longer felt real. The condemned man was desperately trying to clutch at his throat as if he believed that he could stop the immense flow of blood. It was futile of course.

A fast flowing river of deep crimson spilled forth onto the carpet creating a thick and sticky pool which stank of impending death. Tyler looked straight into his father's eyes, defiantly watching the final ebb and flow of life drain away from the figure who had created him. He knew he ought to have felt some guilt for what he'd just done, but he couldn't bring himself to affect even a sliver of empathy.

He never thought of the fact that having recently lost one parent, he had just sent his other parent to join them. In his mind, his mother was a saint and this black-hearted figure did not deserve to share the same ethereal space as her. Tyler must have sat there motionless for at least 5 minutes. The twitching corpse of his father lay at his feet, the ruby red puddle of congealed blood ran around the edges of his shoes. It was going to be one hell of a mess for some poor soul to clean up.

It was obvious that he couldn't stay there. How the hell could he have possibly explained it away? "Well, officer it's like this you see. My father was spoiling for a fight, so I slashed his throat open to teach him a bit of a lesson and wouldn't you know it - he bled to death right here in front of me!" No, he had to get the hell out of there and fast.

He went and quickly grabbed a rucksack from his bedroom, rapidly stuffing a few essentials into it: a large bottle of water, four cereal bars, a swiss army knife, a powerbank, a tin opener and two sets of clothes. It wasn't much but it was better than nothing. His mind was all a buzz and he found himself in a deep fog of confusion. He also took the liberty of relieving his father of his wallet which contained $350 in cash. He didn't know how far he would get with that sum, but being an exceptionally resourceful young man, he had been taught the principles of thrift and economy by his mother.

Leaving the house and making no attempt to cover his tracks, he made his way hurriedly and short of breath to the bus station where he purchased a ticket to a far off town named Prince Albert. Pulling into the bus terminal, it looked to him even more of a one-horse town than the one he had come from, but there was method in his madness.

Known as the 'Gateway to the North' there lay a vast and expansive national park just beyond the town and that was where he was headed. Better to hide out and give the cops something to do than simply surrender and make it easy for them. He knew now that he was a fallen angel and there would be no redemption.

Other than stealing quietly into the gaping hinterland, no plan existed in his mind. He was simply planting one foot in front of the other and taking things down to their most basic level. The universe could decide his fate as far as he was concerned.

Casting a concerned glance in his direction, the bus driver called after young Tyler and asked who was coming to meet him. Tyler grinned sheepishly back at him and said that his uncle Burt would be driving to collect him the next morning. The driver had a kindly, avuncular look about him. Sage brown eyes and a compassionate smile spoke of a guy who had likely lived a modest, small town life yet seen and shown friendliness to many people over his years. The older gentleman simply shrugged and said "OK, kid," bading him good luck.

Despite his tender age, Tyler looked a couple of years older than he was, so the curiosity which you might expect an 11-year-old to arouse had a more limited impact than it might otherwise have.

Besides, this was a small town and thoughts of crime and abduction were more than likely far from most of the locals' thoughts. Slipping a truck driver $40 and asking him to look the other way whilst he hitched a ride up front in the cab to Tyler's surprise, actually worked.

They headed north up highway 2 for just over an hour before the boy politely asked if he could take his leave at the next truckstop. The driver seemingly had little interest in who this young man was, let alone concern for his welfare. He was just happy to receive a few notes in exchange for a temporary passenger. No questions asked. It suited him just fine.

Saying goodbye to the gruff truck driver at a desolate gas station miles from anywhere, Tyler realised just how far away from anywhere he was.

There was no way back for him now and certainly no prospect of a normal life waiting for him back in civilization. The best he could hope for would either be life in a brutal borstal or some kind of young offenders institute. Could he even countenance it? Not a chance. He would prefer to meet his end as a free spirit, que sera, sera.

So that was precisely what led him to be standing right here facing this shimmering, majestic lake. The water was the colour of sapphire, almost perfectly still and lying like some infinite mirror that reflected the endless sky. Thousands upon thousands of mighty evergreens framed the breathtaking picture set out before him.

He had managed to quell his rising panic, but bigger problems lay close at hand. He was starving, cold and rootless. There was no longer any script to follow and he was truly alone in the world. The epic depth of the lake and the fathomless emptiness of his surroundings simply mirrored his overwhelming sense of insignificance.

Shapes and colours began to dance in front of his eyes. Paranoia rapped at the door and demanded to be let in. A sense of numbness took hold of him with a vice-like icy grip. Out of nowhere, he felt a hot breath on the back of his neck. He spun around and with a gasping cry found himself standing in front of a grizzly bear. This was the moment of departure, he felt.

Closing his eyes, he braced himself. Make it quick, please God. Yet, nothing happened. He slowly opened his eyes again. The grizzly bear raised a paw. Five claws glinted menacingly in the wintry sunshine. Tyler by this point was feeling more dazed as the seconds went by and had no idea how to react to the bizarre spectacle unfolding in front of him.

The cold was steadily penetrating all of his joints and slowly but surely, like a victim clinging to a life raft in an icy river awaiting rescue, the life steadily and inexorably drained out of him, just as it had with his father.

In spite of his fading consciousness, to Tyler's astonishment, the bear spoke up. "You have committed a grave sin, Tyler Beresford." A faint flicker of recognition registered in the boy's eyes. In his advanced state of a wilting descent toward mortality, it didn't strike him as particularly odd that a giant grizzly bear should be speaking to him.

The big animal continued his final sermon. "Even so, you had your reasons for committing this act. It is important that I pass on a message to you from your mother." His mother? Now he had the strength to hang on, if only for a little bit longer. He wanted to hear this important message. "She wants you to know that she loves you and that you are forgiven. Therefore, there is only one thing left for me to do."

Tyler was by now in the final throes of hypothermia. He forced himself to speak, slurred though his speech was. "What was it?" he enquired of the talking Grizzly. Tyler could have sworn that he observed a trace of regret in the bear's manner at this point. He held off the oncoming spell of death with all the courage and determination he could muster.

He needn't have exerted himself so. In the mere blink of an eye, the bear had brought down his blade like claws and slashed them diagonally across the boy's neck in a perfect replication of the earlier killing of his own father.

Tyler's beast of burden was released and his pain was no more. The picture postcard scene grew sullied with that strange foreign object. Blood oozed, incongruous across the bank of the river, trickling along like a claret coloured snake in hiding. The boy was reunited with his mother once more; the deep blue river merely yawned and looked on impassively.

AN UNEXPECTED PASSENGER

Straight as an arrow, the thin wedge of tarmac stretched all the way out to the horizon, as far as the eye could see. Encased by towering, distant mountains and flanked on both sides by an unbroken, dusty desert, the reddish lunar landscape spoke of another world.

Drumming her fingers steadily on the steering wheel to the beat of "Stuck in the Middle with You," she kept her eyes fixed on the road ahead, pondering that song's discomposed lyrics. *Well I don't know why I came here tonight. I've got the feeling that something ain't right.*

Recalling from a distant corner of her memory where she might have heard that song before, it came to her teasingly and by degrees. That was it! It was from a Quentin Tarantino movie. Which one was it? *Pulp Fiction? Kill Bill?* No, it wasn't either of them.

She pondered further, with plenty of time and space in which to ruminate. Of course. It was *Reservoir Dogs*. That sense of satisfaction that can only come from triumphantly reeling in a particularly evasive nugget of information lying tantalisingly just out of reach, washed over her.

A mile or so up ahead, she could just make out a distant figure, dressed apparently in all white. The unknown apparition stood out markedly against the clay red landscape and she crinkled her nose in confusion.

There were no other cars in sight in her line of sight, despite the arrow-like road running for many miles in both directions like a thin black strip of liquorice stretching into infinity.

A kindly individual who regularly gave to charity and believed in the principle of "turning the other cheek," she always sought to treat others with patience and compassion and felt a prick of concern for the mysterious speck in the distance.

There and then, she made a decision. She would help this person if he required it. Others wouldn't have given it a second thought and would have had no intention of stopping to help their fellow human being. Sure, she had heard of many stories about dangerous hitchhikers often suggesting that picking one up was to invite danger, but what did they *really* know?

Probably just scaremongering. The song continued. *"I got the feeling that something ain't right. I'm so scared in case I fall off my chair."* The car continued to zip along, the engine humming contentedly. The outside temperature reading currently sat at 35c. It was at times like these that she was glad to have air conditioning. 'That poor person,' she thought to herself. 'They must be sweltering in this heat.'

She began to feel a strong sense of comfort that she would be able to offer this person some refuge from the baking sun as well as a lift in the direction they were presumably headed.

She was now perhaps just half a mile from the unidentified hitchhiker. As the car drew closer, she deduced that it was a man, from his gait perhaps an older gentleman, dressed in what appeared from a far distance to be an all-white suit.

She could also now see that he was wearing what looked like a brown Homburg hat and was standing stock still. She thought it was strange that he wasn't at the very least holding out his thumb or making some kind of gesture to indicate that he was seeking a ride.

The man just stood and stared vacantly in her direction. Many might have felt unsettled, but our humanitarian crusader merely continued, fixed steadfastly on her mission, guiding the car effortlessly to where the man stood by the roadside. His expression inscrutable, a cloud of dust rose as the vehicle pulled in and rolled to a stop.

Lowering the passenger side window via an electric button, she decided to try and break the ice. "Do you need a lift?" The gentleman wore a look that was at once curious and friendly, bemused and tolerant. His weathered face was lined by the passage of time and his skin was composed of a healthy complexion that seemed to have spent a significant amount of time in the sun.

His straight shoulder length hair, silver in colour gave him the air of a guru-like character and he could easily have passed for a TV evangelist on some ghastly daytime talk show. A welcoming smile slowly broke out across his face.

The gentleman possessed a pair of pale blue eyes that at once pierced their subject yet not in a threatening manner, more in the sense that you somehow felt that you were in the presence of wisdom and learned gravitas.

"As a matter of fact, I am," replied the man in a deep and resonant drawl, the root of which she couldn't quite place. Momentarily transfixed by the aura of those aquamarine eyes, she regained her composure. "Well, I'm heading west if that's any use?" "Thank you, that would be very helpful."

She noticed that he didn't appear to be carrying any luggage with him, not even a bag by the looks of it. "Aren't you carrying anything with you? A bag, perhaps?" she ventured, not knowing whether it was polite or intrusive to venture such enquiries into a stranger's plans.

"Just myself," he replied somewhat indulgently, omitting any requirement for superfluous conversation. He certainly didn't seem the type to *dance around the handbags* when it came to verbal interaction.

Finally breaking eye contact after what seemed longer than what might constitute normal, he looked both ways up and down the road, as if to check that there was no other human being in visible existence for the nearest 5 miles or so.

Satisfied that this indeed appeared to be the case, he reached out a bony hand, dotted with an array of faded freckles and pulled the metal handle, opening the car door. High above them in the cavernous blue sky, the sun blazed down with ferocious energy.

While its rays glinted off the chrome trim of the window frame, dazzling her and forcing her to squint, she had the vague feeling that some of that blinding light could actually be resonating from her new companion himself. The man seemed to glide into the car with the grace of a ballet dancer, there was no heavy thump as he landed in his seat, rather it was a lithe movement that seemed effortless.

He closed the door gently, the action making a soft clunk. It was hard to explain, but to her the man seemed to exude a wonderful sense of calmness. She felt instantly at ease in his presence. Any sense of danger evaporated into thin air and she felt that her role of the good samaritan was vindicated.

Turning to her with a warm smile and the traces of a far-off twinkle in his eye, he interlaced his fingers and rested his chain above them. "Well, shall we move on?" Nodding, she took her foot off the brake pedal and the engine rumbled back into life once again. Rediscovering her appetite for friendly conversation, she proffered a hand, whilst keeping the other on the steering wheel.

"I'm Jessica." He glanced at the extended hand as if unsure as to what he should do with it before volunteering his own and connecting with a gentle, but assertive handshake. "It's nice to meet you, Jessica." Casting brief glances in his direction, flitting her eyes between him and the empty road ahead, she paused expectantly for him to offer his own name by reply.

Instead, he simply smoothed out the creases in his linen trousers and in a quiet voice said "it's probably better to keep your eyes on the road, Jessica." This advice seemed tongue-in-cheek and she took no great offence at it, although she considered it ever so slightly rude considering that she was doing him a favour and not the other way around.

The car continued to traverse the barren desert and they were both silent for a time. Eventually, the silence was broken. "So, you are on a journey are you not?" enquired the man in the white suit. "Who isn't?" retorted Jessica, a touch prickly. The gentleman simply ignored the latent trace of irritation and pursued his line of enquiry. "But what are you looking for? That's the real question, is it not?"

She scrunched up her nose unconsciously at his manner of speaking. It sounded to her almost like he was from a different time. It brought to mind the way a Dickensian character might construct their sentences. "To tell you the truth..." she began. "I have a motto which I live by: Live and let live. It's a pretty simple philosophy, but it makes sense to me."

Nodding firmly at this assertion, she drummed her fingers on the steering wheel before continuing. "I also believe that we should all learn to live in harmony with another. Humanity, I mean." The gentleman tilted his head to the side and pouted his lips as though he was giving deep thought and consideration to what the lady was saying.

"Admirable sentiments," he offered. Although he hadn't meant it to sound flippant, Jessica took it as such. "You think I'm naive, right? Just a gullible, god fearing Christian lady?" She continued nodding robotically as she always did when angered by something.

"I make no such judgements, Jessica. Only God can judge." "Then we're at least agreed on that," she exclaimed, her anger dissolving all at once, a beam on her face at this reassuring return to cordiality. "I had no awareness of your religion by the way," offered the gentleman as a softener. "That's because my crucifix is in the glovebox," replied Jessica bursting into good natured peals of laughter. A hint of a smile played at the corners of the man's mouth, but he did not permit himself any greater expression of merriment.

After Jessica's laughter had faded away, he picked up the conversation. "I have met disciples of many different faiths along my journey, Jessica. Christians, like yourself. Muslims, Buddhists, Jews, Hindus, Sikhs, Confucianists, even Scientologists! But you know, in the end, when all's said and done - there are just two fundamental concepts that we need to understand whilst we are here on earth - *love and fear*."

Jessica looked at him askance. He pressed on regardless. "Every human being is on their own individual journey. As they go through life, when all is said and done, their sole and fundamental task is to *reduce their fears* and *increase their level of love*." He paused for a moment to observe her reaction. She seemed intrigued by where this was all going, so he continued.

"We have all agreed to undertake this long journey together. No matter which religion you subscribe to, or as the case might be, if you have made the choice not to follow religion of any kind, every life has a purpose. There are no wasted lessons, even when we want to shake our fist at the sky and angrily proclaim to our god how unfair life is, there is ultimately a meaningful purpose to every shred of pain we experience, just as there is joy in every happy experience."

Jessica took this all in, running her index finger down the bridge of her nose in contemplation. "You have a nice way of looking at the world, mister," she offered, cautiously. He ran his thumb over the back of his hand in circles, as if considering how to phrase his response.

"It's not something you can share with everybody, I know that much. Reactions can range from confusion, through bewilderment to outright hostility, depending on the age of that person's soul." Jessica did a double take. "The age of a person's soul...come again?"

"Let me try and explain how this all works. Please don't freak out and crash the car, or worse yet, leave me stranded at a service station." Although he had attempted to lighten the mood with this witticism, Jessica was clearly too distracted, too perturbed by the content of their dialogue that he saw it would have made no sense to draw her attention to his poor joke. Observing her bemusement, he pressed on.

"The number seven plays a major role in this journey. There are seven soul roles, seven characteristics of fear, seven goals of development, seven modes, seven mentalities, seven centres, seven soul ages, seven soul ages and seven stages of development. In simple terms, every individual fragment possesses their own soul matrix which provides what is effectively a map of their own unique make-up. Before embarking upon this long journey, each soul family, which consists of multiple fragments and entities, agreed to undertake the long cycle of reincarnation through which we must advance via 35 levels of increased consciousness before we cycle off and return to the causal world."

Jessica simply stared straight ahead, an expression of perfect bewilderment on her face. It was a good 30 seconds or so before she composed a reply to this unexpected torrent of theorems.

"The bible doesn't cite the existence of reincarnation. So I find it hard to believe in, sorry. Besides, that theory of yours wouldn't apply to me. We're only here once, everyone knows that." The gentleman in the white suit merely smiled to himself.

"I'm not here to try and persuade you otherwise. This is not some cult religion. Blind faith is not required since you can quite easily apply the framework to any one person's individual situation and from there, it's up to them whether they can derive true benefit from it or otherwise. Every single individual here on earth has fears, let me tell you. There is not a shadow of doubt about that. How do you think wars start? What common denominator drives dictators the world over?"

"Maybe so, but you're actually suggesting that we have to keep coming back? Where is the fun in that? Trying to be a good person and getting into heaven sounds more like my cup of tea. Doing it over and over again just sounds like a punishment." He shot back at her: "You chose this journey. You chose your parents, the country you were incarnated in - the vast majority of the people you have met or will meet in this life. Most of it was pre-planned, although there is of course a certain amount of free will and room to make different choices or take alternative paths."

She looked even more confused now. "I chose my parents? What's all that about?" The gentleman merely gave a curt nod. "Yes, you did." Jessica's face contorted in disgust. "My mother treated me like dirt. She never wanted me. Never offered me comfort when I needed it.

That's why I left home as soon as I was able to. I resolved to find god and by extension, inner peace. I determined that I would treat people with kindness and warmth just as my mother had failed to do so with me." Jessica had become rather worked up during this outburst and blew a large puff of air out of her cheeks as if to try and reset herself. The gentleman could clearly see that the woman's painful memories were quite genuine.

"Try to look at this way. "It's entirely possible that you chose this mother to learn certain life lessons and to overcome fears that needed to be transmuted," he suggested, gently. Jessica grew pensive at this. They were silent for some moments before the gentleman spoke again. "The godly principle is love and understanding. Love merges with understanding in the godly."

His words filtered slowly through the cool, air-conditioned cabin of the car and step by step, formed some kind of impression on her.

"You mentioned soul roles...what do you mean exactly? These people are set certain tasks... Is that right?" He cracked his knuckles gently in a non-intrusive way before continuing. "Well, as I mentioned, there are seven different soul roles. Each of them have certain energies, as well as attributes and weaknesses. They are, in order, the Healer, the Artist, the Warrior, the Scholar, the Sage, the Priest and the King. You can expect Healers to be very oriented toward the service of others, they are often caring and compassionate.

Think of Mother Teresa for example." Seeing that he had her attention, he continued to expound. "Artists are naturally creative and feel compelled to create, to express. Vincent van Gogh is the archetypal example of such a soul role. Warriors as you might expect are driven by the principle of fighting. Let's just say that if there were no Warriors in this world, the desire for progress and change would be lacking. They are never truly at peace. Scholars as you can expect are driven by the principles of learning and teaching. Beethoven was a Scholar as was Shakespeare."

Jessica whistled out loud. What had seemed up until about 10 minutes ago was no longer an uneventful journey. She had to admit to herself that she was enjoying the discussion despite the internal conflicts she felt as she chewed over the old man's deeply held convictions. He continued to elucidate. "Then you have the Sage, who is all about communication. They are often talkative and always expressive. Quite often, famous actors and actresses are Sages. Some examples are George Clooney, Tom Hanks, Christopher Walken, Jennifer Aniston, Julia Roberts. There are many examples in this particular field." "Makes sense," interjected Jessica.

They passed a giant billboard informing them of a service station situated 12 miles up the highway. "Energy number 6 is held by the Priest. These souls are driven by a desire to provide consolation, which means that at their best, they are compassionate, at their worst, they are zealots. Gandhi was one. John Lennon another - you can perhaps feel it in the songs he wrote and his later activism. A more recent example of an influential Priest is Barack Obama."

Raising her eyebrows at this modern example, he met her eyes with a sudden look of seriousness. "All of these soul roles have positive and negative poles, you know. One useful exercise you can do on a regular basis for yourself is to simply sit and observe what you are doing. Ask yourself if you are acting out of love, or out of fear. Are you currently in your positive pole or your negative pole?" She began to nod, as though there was method to his madness, shocking to her though his new age-like theory seemed.

"The seventh role is that of the King. There aren't many who have the soul role of the King," he said, nodding thoughtfully. They operate from the principle of leading and providing leadership. At their best, they are dignified, at their worst tyrannical." "If there are so few of these kings, how can you tell them apart from other profiles?" enquired Jessica, with growing interest in the theme.

"The eyes of the king are cold and sharply focused, with a commanding look in the gaze that feels solid and grounded. The energy may seem imposing at first, even uncompromising, but that's because the regal look of the king is weighted with authority. A king can fill a room whether they want to or not, they don't have to do anything to draw attention to themself - they cannot easily be overlooked. Steve Jobs was a King, as was JFK."

He paused as if to reflect. The scorched, dusty landscape around them remained unaltered and the ancient craggy mountains which seemed to have been there for millenia stood majestically as if to remind them of their own impermanence as humans, their entire lives effectively passing in the blink of an eye when compared to the unfathomable timespan of those natural wonders.

"I'm not here to freak you out, Jessica. You seem to me like a very decent person. Your life motto clearly spells that out. You have made it your mission to treat others with patience, respect and compassion. These are truly wonderful qualities and I wholeheartedly recommend that you continue being kind to others. I cannot promise obviously that you will not encounter ups and downs in your life - quite the opposite, however - use those experiences! People will come into your life who appear on the surface hell bent on causing problems and trying to hurt you, but I can assure you if it can be of any comfort that these are actually angels for you.

It's probably reverse logic to think of it that way, but consider this. The enemies you encounter in this life might be those which you have pre-existing agreements with. Are you familiar with the concept of karma?" She nodded in the affirmative.

The gentleman appeared to brush off a few imaginary crumbs from his lapels. "My advice is to try and fix the relationship with your mother." Jessica began to sob and dabbed the corner of her eyes with the back of her hand. "It's OK to cry. Into every life, some rain must fall. Better to express than to repress." He chuckled inwardly at the inadvertent rhyme he created.

"Not everyone is ready to hear what I've relayed to you. Not until Mature 5 at least." Even if she didn't quite comprehend his meaning, Jessica sniffed loudly and declared that she felt better now.

"There's just one small but important saying I want you to remember after we have parted today. *No rain, no rainbows.*" She smiled through puffy, red-eyes at him. His aquamarine specimens returned her smile with genuine warmth. Pointing up ahead, the man in the white suit changed the subject. "Jessica, if it's not inconvenient to you, I'd like to walk the last few miles up to the service station." Expressing her usual compassion, she adopted a look of concern in trying to ascertain whether he was 100% sure. He put her mind at rest with self-assured declarations of being fully accustomed to the hot son, feeling as did so for his hat. Finding that it was still perched on the top of his head, Jessica pulled the car over to the side of the road as requested.

They were still quite a distance from civilisation, but she didn't protest any further, recognising that he was ready to make his own way from here. Gliding back out of the car and touching his hand to the brim of his hat in an old-fashioned gesture of chivalry, he gave her one last, examining look. "Remember what I said. *No rain, no rainbows.*" She nodded earnestly at him. "I won't forget."

She pulled back out onto the road, alone once again, the cabin eerily quiet and noticeably empty of the former presence of her unexpected passenger. She looked in the rear view mirror but to her surprise, the gentleman in the white suit was gone. Her mysterious messenger had vanished for all time.

IN COLOGNE'S CATHEDRAL

It had been a long day. The businessman arrived home just after 8pm and threw his keys into a bowl that rested on the kitchen worktop. He wasn't particularly hungry - more fatigued - and felt the need for a drink and some quiet reflection. Loosening his tie and unbuttoning the top of his shirt, he strolled across to the drinks cabinet and selected a half-empty bottle of Laphroaig which a former love interest had bought for him the previous year.

Pouring himself two fingers of scotch and tossing in a single ice cube, the words of Mark Twain came to his mind. "Too much of anything is bad, but too much good whiskey is barely enough." Snorting loudly at the wisdom of that celebrated mind, he made his way over to the wingback armchair that was as comfortable and soothing as the arms of a loving woman and eased into a sprawl. Sipping his scotch, he allowed the peaty, richness of the flavour glide down his throat satisfyingly. Thoughts of work and boardroom struggles invaded his newfound serenity and he made a conscious effort to push them away. It was no good, he would need to find an aid through which he could switch off and enter a different headspace.

He pulled a pair of expensive Sony headphones over his ears and called out to his voice activated smart home system to fire up

Spotify. It wasn't immediately clear to him what he should listen to. Was he looking for the sunshine and simplicity of Mozart, the poetry of Chopin, the triumph over adversity of Beethoven or the aggression of Wagner?

In the end, he tried a different tack. "Play something by Schumann!" he commanded his AI powered assistant. Through the use of algorithms designed by far cleverer people than he, the system opted for a randomly generated track which turned out to be the 4th movement of Schumann's Rhenish symphony, performed in this recording by the NDR Sinfonieorchester with Christopher Eschenbach conducting.

The orchestra entered his ears with a bleak, shivering Eb minor chord. He was instantly transported into a different sphere of existence. Entitled *Feierlich*, a German word meaning solemnly, this movement was certainly aptly named. The businessman closed his eyes and listened to the trombones and French horns recite the hauntingly quiet opening chorale.

The smoky scotch swirled around his mouth and lent an extra bite to the effects of the music. He had read somewhere that the composer had based this entire symphony around the famous river Rhine and that this movement was actually meant to represent the magnificent cathedral that stands on the banks of that river in the city of Cologne. Apparently the construction work had taken 800 years to complete, which surely only added to the majesty of mystique of the vast building. It must have witnessed so much history throughout its existence, so many people passing through over the intervening centuries.

Allowing the music to wash over him as though he were in a Turkish bath, the businessman drifted along with the tide and strongly felt each deep emotion contained within the score. Lush strings began to overlap with one another, the music becoming more profound and the meaning ever more mysterious.

Thoughts of his daily grind and corporate struggles evaporated and it seemed as though he was being carried off in a new direction on the crest of a wave. There was no strength in his body, nor desire to protest and he slowly entered into a new realm. It was as though he had been hypnotised. He couldn't seem to rouse himself from his stupor.

Just then, he was jolted out of his reverie by an unexpected fanfare of trumpets. Opening his eyes, with a panic he realised that he was no longer at home in his easy chair. Grasping for answers and trying to make sense of the visual transformation in front of him, he seemed inexplicably to have gone back in time.

The people all around him were dressed in mid-19th century clothing. They were all regarding him with varying degrees of curiosity, wariness and suspicion. How had he got here? Was his mind playing tricks on him?

Attempting to feel for his now absent headphones, he touched his ears involuntarily, causing a woman nearby to abruptly stand up and walk away. Dressed in a modern business suit, he must have looked particularly out of place. It made no sense - he could still hear the trumpets playing in unison.

Then he realised. He was in a church, or perhaps a cathedral. Glancing around, he took in the sheer scale of the place and marvelled at the height of the ceiling. It *had to be* a cathedral.

Emanating from the very rear of this great edifice, he suddenly realised the source of the music - an orchestra was playing in the distance, the sound reverberating around the cavernous building. The music which he thought was coming from his now absent headphones was actually emanating from the orchestra playing in front of him.

Some kind of ceremony involving an archbishop and a cardinal appeared to be underway and there was an almost oppressive air of solemnity pervading the scene.

From his position, he tried to survey the man who was conducting the orchestra. With a jolt, he realised that he was looking at Robert Schumann directing the assembled musicians. His mouth dropped open in shock. It couldn't be? He glanced a little to the side and saw a lady sitting in a chair nearby, observing the conductor and realised with a gulp that it had to be the famous composer's wife, Clara Schumann.

It was unmistakably the lady from all those black and white photographs. He felt queasy all of a sudden and had to grab onto the back of the next pew to prevent himself from toppling over.

An angry hissing directed at him in guttural German was audible underneath the sound of the orchestra and to his deep embarrassment, the famous conductor glanced in his direction with a severe, admonishing look. He wished that the floor could swallow him up so that he might escape this bizarre and unsettling scene.

Trying to quell the rising panic, he gripped the wooden pew and tightly screwed his eyes closed. The music remained with him, winding down with an air of grim resignation, however when he chanced to open his eyes once again, he found himself back in the safe harbour of his easychair.

His heart thumping, he felt immense relief washing over him. Picking up the now empty glass of Laphroaig and with a suspicious sideways glance at it, he shook his head and reflected on the peculiarities of cognitive function.

A VIGILANTE IN
OUR MIDST

It was the final straw. She'd had enough. The time for mealy mouthed appeasement and constant pandering to the parents of contemptuous, feral children was over. It was time to take matters into her own hands.

At just 14 years old, Holly Broadtower was a formidable young woman. A yellow belt in karate with her eyes firmly set on achieving her next (green) belt within the coming months, she already held firm convictions as to what was right and what was wrong in this world.

Treating people with kindness and generosity, being a decent human and taking decisive action against those who wished to do her and her family harm formed part of her core beliefs. If there was one thing she couldn't stand, it was bullies.

She held a deep and visceral hatred of them. They were found in every walk of life, she knew, and it was unfortunately a part of human nature which no amount of do-gooding and well-meant intention would seemingly ever eradicate, yet she felt *compelled* to take action against any such behaviour when she saw it.

'It isn't possible to be the world's policeman, Holly,' her Sensei had told her more than once, but when she saw injustice, there was no way she could comfortably sit idly by.

For that reason, she had been embroiled in several fights at school, her parents called in repeatedly to attend a series of solemn meetings with the headteacher who, it was clear, was of an appeasement-first mentality rather than the decisive, action oriented kind.

Holly's frequent crusades for justice were tempered by the fact that she had never actively sought out a fight nor, truth be told, started one herself. These incidents had invariably broken out on account of her defending the victim of an unprovoked attack by a gang of bullies; in such situations, Holly felt that she had had little choice but to use force in order to defend both herself and the victim.

Further complicating the picture was the fact that her parents, who had separated when she was five years old, saw things very differently. Her father proudly championed his daughter's bravery in the face of such cowardice on the bullies part - and in his private view, the headteacher - whilst her mother routinely scolded and admonished her for getting involved in other people's quarrels and becoming entangled in such troublesome exploits.

She was a fearless young woman and felt burning indignation at the continuing inaction on the part of the school to do anything meaningful that might have put a decisive stop to the bullying. It pained her that no-one appeared capable of taking the perpetrators' parents to task on their abject failure to teach their children about how to behave properly.

Whilst it's true that those who subjected their prey to such vindictive torture were both wary and cautious of Holly, like all bullies they were themselves mere cowards who sought safety in numbers and tended to hang around in gangs, intimidating those they identified as weaker than themselves.

To date, Holly had been involved in at least four incidents where she had been drawn into these conflicts and had fought off bullies who had singled out their target. On each of those occasions, she had not been actively involved, simply walking along minding her own business, but hearing the shouts and screams of some poor victim and seeing that no-one else had bothered to come to their aid, she had purposefully waded in - risking injury in the process.

The motley crew were led by a ringleader called Bella Mayfield, a 15 year old from a broken home with a mean, pinched face and cold, dark eyes who seemed incapable of constructing a simple sentence without embellishing her speech with an ugly, coarse smattering of expletives. This was someone who carried a near constant look of scornful contempt around with them.

Bella and her cronies had quickly developed a withering disdain for Holly on account of her bravery and the fact that she was the only person in the entire school - teaching staff included - with the guts to stand up to her and her lackeys.

It seemed as though the school was more concerned with protecting their upwardly mobile reputation than allowing such unsavoury incidents to rear their ugly head, and so they proceeded to sweep such iniquities under the proverbial carpet at the earliest opportunity.

On all previous occasions, the victims of the pernicious Bella and her gang had been mere acquaintances of Holly, none of them being particularly close to her. Until today that is. They had made a big mistake. Holly had a cousin named Jim who lived in the next town who had Down's Syndrome.

He was a 10 year old boy who received additional support at his school and as a result, Holly felt especially responsible for his well being. The two of them got on very well and had spent a lot of time playing together when they were younger. That afternoon, Jim had been driven up to the school by his mother in order to meet Holly at the gates by way of surprise.

Neither Jim nor his mother were aware that Holly was being kept in school detention for her involvement in defending a classmate who had been attacked earlier that week and would not be released for another half an hour.

She had neglected to tell her mother with whom she lived for fear of causing her worry, so instead had said that she would walk into town with her friends after school to hang out in a coffee shop. Bella and her gang didn't know who the unusual looking boy standing inside the school gates was, but to them he looked different and that was enough to warrant setting upon him.

Like a pack of wolves they made for him, eyes unwaveringly fixed upon him at all times, encircling the boy who, in his innocence remained completely unaware of their intentions. He blinked at the menacing looking crew of girls who surrounded him with mocking, derisory expressions that to him felt strangely cold and unkind. He didn't understand why.

"Hey spastic!" yelled Bella at the child, cackles of laughter emanating throughout the group. Jim was taken aback. He wasn't accustomed to hearing such terms thrown at him. "Oi. I'm talking to you, dickhead," snarled Bella. Pointing a tobacco stained index finger directly at him, other members of this nasty faction chimed in. "Maybe he can't hear us? What are you retarded AND deaf, mate?"

Jim's heart began to beat like the clappers. He wanted to run away. Where was his cousin? She would protect him. "Look at him! Little shit probably wants to piss his pants," bellowed another callous voice. "What's wrong with your eyes, bruv?" Poor Jim sensed deep danger and decided to make a run for it. There were no clear means of escape, but he felt an increasing desperation which was scaring him intensely.

Given that he was much shorter than all the girls who stood in a circle around him, he charged directly at the midriff of the one who appeared to be the ringleader. He collided roughly with her stomach and bounced off her like a ball against a wall and fell back, helplessly into the circle. "Give him a good kicking, girls!" barked Bella and a chorus of blows rained down upon Jim's body. He was utterly terrified and had no means of escaping the ordeal.

Mercilessly, the girls took it in turns to bring their feet down upon his prostrate form, stamping all over him, one or two of them deriving a kind of sick thrill from their savagery. Jim experienced pain like he'd never known before and his mind raced to try and understand what was happening to him.

There was no letting up - even when one of the girls apparently tired, there was another to take over the incessant hitting and trampling. No mercy was shown. Jim started to lose consciousness when in the far off distance, barely audible he could hear the weak, apologetic voice of the school's headteacher calling out. "Stop that, please. That's enough, now. Come away, please." The girls rapidly dispersed and ran away before the ineffective figure shuffled toward the scene of the beating.

To his disquiet, he observed the battered and pathetic looking figure of a young boy sprawled out on the ground, writhing in agony from the effects of his assault. Glancing nervously around with darting eyes to find out whether anyone was watching, the headteacher called out and gestured to a gathering of students across the field who were kicking a football around between them.

They started to make their way nonchalantly toward where the headteacher stood by the school gates. It was clear that he had

31

little authority, even less respect. After what seemed like an age, they finally arrived. "Here, help this young man up. It looks like a misunderstanding of some kind…Jones - can you go and fetch the school nurse please?" Jones, a gangly student with a laconic expression turned and slowly made his way back to the main building to seek out the nurse, assuming that she hadn't finished for the day.

Just then, Jim's mother came racing up to the group, a look of fury mixed with disbelief etched into her expression. "What the *hell* has happened here?" She looked angrily at the weak faced headteacher, demandingly before kneeling down to attend to her son. He was still conscious, but badly bruised and carrying a resigned air of confusion, as though he was totally unable to process what had just happened to him.

Fifteen minutes later, Jim and his mother were sitting across from the headteacher in his study. Flustered, stammering his apologies, protesting that he couldn't possibly understand for one moment what had happened and that in his school nothing remotely like this had ever happened before, the door suddenly burst open with some force.

Standing there was the crimson faced Holly, fists clenched, apoplectic with bottled rage. "I heard what happened," she said, shaking with indignation, looking directly into the headteacher's eyes with unwavering power. Her eyes remained fixed on him for a good 10 seconds before she finally broke contact and raced over to her cousin who had recovered sufficiently to have calmly taken a seat and sip a glass of water.

He looked terrible. His face was black and blue, there were cuts all over his hands where those cowards had presumably jumped up and down on him and presumably underneath his clothes, there was far worse damage that had yet to meet the eye. Jim's mother, who was taken aback by the way that Holly had apparently shattered the expected protocol by storming into this office and who it must be said had no existing knowledge of the unchallenged bullying that went on in this school, stared agape at Holly.

Looking up at the headteacher from where she knelt down beside Jim, she spoke with authority that belied her years. "What are you going to do about it? They keep getting away with it! Never again." The headteacher, seeing that any authority he supposedly held by dint of his position was severely threatened, spoke up. "Now, look here, Holly…" She cut him off with a raised hand. "This is the last straw, sir. If you're not willing to do something about those *bitches*, I will!"

Jim's mother winced at her coarse language, but understood deep down that she spoke out of passion and righteous indignation. It was her turn to contribute to the awkward exchange. "Do I take it to understand sir, that bullying is permitted in this school?"

Hearing this, the headteacher blanched and spluttered in his chair, desperately searching for the words with which he had rebuked such accusations hundreds of times in the past, only this time none would come. It was one thing having pupils squabbling amongst themselves, but having a 10 year old boy with Down's syndrome beaten by a pack of feral teenage girls at the school gates was utterly inexcusable.

He pondered briefly whether he might somehow bribe them or attempt to persuade them by charm to not reveal any of this to outside sources. "Look," he said, avoiding eye contact with this headstrong young lady. "Holly. Why don't you take tomorrow off? It's Friday after all. I think it's better that you don't come into contact with Bella and her friends for the next few days."

This only served to infuriate the fiery young woman. "To hell with that. I'll see that she gets what's coming to her. You can count on that." Alarmed at this declaration of intent, the headteacher looked helplessly to Jim's mother for moral support.

She picked up on this and turned to Holly. "Hol, I know how you feel. I'm just as angry as you are, but violence isn't always the answer. If you go and hit them, you're just as bad as they are," she suggested, trying to adopt a reasoning tone. "Sorry, Jill but I don't see it that way. You don't cower to bullies. If you do, they'll just keep coming back. That's why you have to hit them twice as hard. They need to be taught a bloody good lesson!" "Please mind your language, Hol. Jim's sitting right here, you know."

Holly closed her eyes in great concentration and gave a gentle nod of acknowledgment. Taking a long deep breath just as she had learned to do many times in her karate classes, she felt instantly calmer and took her leave without a word.

As she walked away, though she had taken a moment to steady herself, the anger remained inside her, burning at the injustice of this feeble, pathetic man in allowing those inhuman, disgusting bullies to get away with it time and time again. She might have a pass for tomorrow, but it wouldn't go to waste. The time would be used effectively, she decided.

That night, Holly holed herself up in her bedroom thinking long and hard about how she would exact revenge on those who attacked her cousin. Various scenarios drifted through her mind; she examined some of them, discarded others and ultimately decided upon one. It wasn't just about inflicting an equal amount of pain back upon them, it was about teaching them a valuable lesson so that they might glean something useful from what would be a tough experience. Hopefully, she reasoned, the net effect would be that they'd think twice about hurting others again in the future.

It was 11pm when she concluded the construction of her plan and turned out the light. A sense of inner contentment buzzed through her system, leaving a warm glow in her breast.

The next day, she simply went along with the plan set out by the headteacher. He had sent Holly's mother an email the previous evening saying that he had granted Holly the day off on account of her much improved behaviour, a lie which suited her to go along with on this occasion.

She spent the day conserving energy - reading, doing yoga exercises and ate a simple lunch of caesar salad and carrot juice. When the appointed time of 2.45pm arrived, she slunk out of the house wearing a low profile dark tracksuit, baseball cap and running shoes, then made her way to the external fringes of school waiting out of sight at a safe distance for her quarry to exit the school gates.

Sure enough, there was Bella Mayfield striding casually down the school drive, flanked as usual by her entourage. They hung on her every word and followed her like sheep, apparently unable to think for themselves. Holly was conscious of a surging in her heart, one that spoke of simmering hostility and again, took a moment to take a few deep breaths and center herself.

As she expected, the gang gradually dispersed and headed off into their different directions, leaving Bella to walk alone. That suited Holly just fine. The ringleader walked with a brash swagger, looking down her nose contemptuously at anyone daring to make eye contact with her. Holly crept out from her vantage point behind the trunk of a thick oak tree and with the stealth of a cheetah stalking a distant gazelle, followed her with cautious steps.

Holly anticipated the route that Bella would take, heading down this main road for approximately 800 yards, before bearing left through a large park and cutting across to the estate where she lived on the far side. Holly didn't intend to let her get that far however.

It proved relatively easy to track the steps of her opponent without allowing her to notice that she was being followed. She would only have had to dodge between the various obstacles on the pavement in the event that Bella should glance back, but in the event she simply looked straight ahead.

Up ahead, she saw Bella dart off to the left and temporarily out of sight into the large park. Holly added some pace to her steps and arriving at the little path that entered the park, peered cautiously around the corner to ascertain that Bella was not looking back. Her luck was holding so far and her hot pursuit had not been noticed.

The park was spread out over an area of approximately 50 acres and it wasn't overly busy; a smattering of mothers with their children, school kids making their way home and the odd older gentleman sitting quietly on one of the many benches. Given the relative scarcity of others around them, Holly felt with an instinctive prick of excitement that now was the time to make her move.

Stealing up behind Bella, she steadied herself and prepared to launch her master plan into action. No-one else was close by and it didn't appear that anyone was looking in their direction. Like a coiled spring, she turned her right hand sideways and applied a devastating karate chop to the back of Bella's neck, rendering her immediately unconscious.

Just as she began to slump to the floor, Holly deftly slipped her arm around Bella's waist and exclaimed faux greetings out loud. "Well, hello Bella! Fancy seeing you here." The pretence was necessary, for if anyone had chanced to look across at the two of them, they would have seen the perfectly normal scene of two friends strolling along in the park, deep in conversation. "You piece of shit," added Holly softly under her breath.

Unsurprisingly, there was no response from her enemy. Fortunately, Holly's extensive training in karate had taught her precisely which points of the body it was possible to manipulate through appropriately directed force and careful manipulation; she knew therefore that there would be no more lasting damage than a bruised ego and indignation on Bella's part when she came to.

Holly hoped however, that this would be just the tip of the iceberg when it came to giving this bully a taste of her own medicine. As she had carefully planned whilst cooped up in her bedroom and studying the local Ordnance Survey map the previous night, there was a secluded copse of trees just up ahead on the left and it was there that she had anticipated executing her own personal brand of retribution.

The area she had in mind was widely regarded by locals as a spot in which various illicit activities took place, many of them pretty unsavoury but mercifully, when she arrived there, dragging Bella along with her, a vice like grip around her waist, there was nobody in there.

Sighing with relief, she allowed herself the pleasure of throwing Bella forcibly down to the ground. Her opponent made very little movement on the ground other than to emit a faint groan of pain.

Moving with the practised efficiency of a ninja, Holly slipped off the rucksack she had been carrying on her shoulders and whipped out of the main zipped pocket a miniature clip on camera. She then proceeded to connect this small device to her smartphone via bluetooth, rendering it completely wireless and opened up Facebook on her phone.

The mild spring night provided ample light for the spectacle that was about to take place and in this quiet, leafy copse, privacy was assured - at least for the time being. Holly squinted with concentration down at her phone screen and hit the "Facebook live" button, commencing a live streaming broadcast from the camera she had pinned to her chest, going out directly to her entire network of friends.

Although she wasn't sure exactly how many friends she had on the platform, she estimated it would have been in the approximate range of 2,000 or so. At the beginning of the live stream there were no viewers - she had not provided any advance warning - but soon enough a steady trickle of interest began to grow like bystanders stopping to gape at an unfolding crime scene.

Bella was just starting to come round and was murmuring deliriously, groaning all the while in discomfort. "What the hell's goin on?" she demanded blinking furiously, annoyed at finding herself face down in what looked like a forest. When she looked up however and realised that she was without the safety of her troupe and facing that nutcase Holly in isolation, her tone changed somewhat.

"You!?" she uttered, with a perfect mixture of fear and insolence. Bristling, Holly marched straight over to her, laid a heavy hand on her head and taking a fistful of hair, yanked her violently to her feet, Bella screaming out loudly all the while. Holly then curled her left fist and delivered a hefty blow to the stomach, causing Bella to promptly collapse at her feet. "Yes, it's me alright. You make another sound and *I will destroy you.*

Nod if you understand," commanded Holly with total authority. Bella had no choice but to do as she was told. "It's not so much fun when the tables are turned, is it, Bella Mayfield?" she asked ironically before landing a full blooded and vicious kick to her abdomen.

A quick glance at her phone screen told her that the number of viewers was up to 27 and accelerating rapidly. Bella couldn't help but let out a yelp at this latest blow and Holly didn't let her off for one second. "I believe I told you NOT TO MAKE ANOTHER SOUND!" hissed the young warrior at the figure withering at her feet in a tone that suggested it would have been extremely foolish to contradict her.

Make that 43 viewers. Holly decided to provide an impromptu running commentary to elucidate to her growing viewership exactly what this intriguing but odd video was all about.

"My name is Holly Broadtower. We are here today to teach this scumbag bully you see here a lesson. After today, she will never again hurt, intimidate or attack another human being." Bella gulped at this. What could she mean by never again? The miniature camera pinned to the front of her tracksuit provided the ever growing audience with a fittingly demeaning view of the newly reduced kingpin. Thumbs up began gliding vertically across the screen accompanied by the occasional emoji.

Holly began to speak once again. "Just yesterday, this disgusting waste of blood and organs along with her bunch of pathetic little cronies proceeded to beat a 10-year-old boy with Down's syndrome to a pulp." You could almost sense the gasps reverberating across cyberspace. "That little boy - Jim is his name - happens to be my cousin."

At this, Holly broke off and rained down a volley of blows with her fists all over Bella's face and body. She thumped her with relentless force, over and over until her enemy was reduced to a whimpering mess on the grass, completely helpless at her feet.

"How does it feel, Bella? Come on, tell everyone. We'd all love to know what little Jim did to deserve such a punishment?" Glowering down at her all the while, no answer was forthcoming, Bella having curled herself up into a ball to try and protect herself for any further strikes.

"Unfortunately for the vast majority of decent kids that attend our school, there is no protection from the adults who are ultimately responsible for that very task. Worse yet, the person who holds that ultimate responsibility, our headteacher is about as much use as a chocolate fireguard." Cue a colourful cascade of *laugh out loud* emojis flooding the screen.

"That's right," she went on, speaking like a fired-up politician who has the bit between their teeth, "This isn't the first time that bullying has taken place in the school. The crying shame is that far from doing anything about it, the powers-that-be have instead tried to shush and downplay any stories that might cause potential embarrassment and make the governors look bad!" She was really hitting her stride now. Bella, peering out furtively from her protective pose, looked white as a sheet amidst this unexpected lesson in oratory.

"Now, I am perfectly aware that I will likely lose my place at the school on account of what I'm doing here tonight, but I'm also someone who believes in principles and protecting those who are picked on by those who would attack them - because they my friends, *they* are the real cowards! Bella Mayfield here (here Holly dished out a sharp and painful kick to the ribs) is the bloody coward! Not my cousin, Jimmy. Not all the other kids who I've tried to protect.

The headteacher should be ashamed of himself. How would he like it if it was his own children that some gang of thugs attacked?" Holly was in full flow now, face flushed with umbrage and chest puffed out like an all conquering hero, meting out her own form of justice, the moral argument in her mind fully justifying her approach.

She crouched down next to the prostrate form of Bella affording, those who were viewing the live stream a closer view of the action. "It looks like someone isn't in the mood for talking. Well, we'll just have to see what we can do to change that."

Her voice trailed off as if deep rumination over how she might make her enemy talk. She didn't have to wait too long before the bully found her voice, much reduced and reedy though it was when it returned. "Please don't hit me any more. I'm sorry, I'm really sorry." Holly seized upon her words immediately. "What are you sorry for?"

Newly contrite, Bella confessed her misdemeanors openly. "For attacking your cousin." Holly wouldn't let her off without a full admission. "Just for my cousin, or?" Bella stammered through her sentences, totally unaccustomed to being the one caught in the trap. How the tables had turned.

"For all of them. I'll never touch anyone again, I swear." "You're damn right you won't. I'll make sure of it," shot back Holly with grit and steel in both word and intent. Bella fully believed her and shuddered at the connotations of what her open threats entailed.

"I'm sure that our live audience would love to hear exactly how people like you come to attack those who simply mind their own businesses. They're no threat to you or your circle whatsoever, yet you choose to set upon them like wild animals, supposedly just for the sheer hell of it." Holly felt herself again getting hot under the collar as she spoke and forced herself to recall the discipline imparted through her karate lessons via the sage words of her sensei himself.

The number of viewers had, remarkably, shot up to 437 in the space of just two minutes. "So come on. Out with it. Why do you feel the need?" Bella had nowhere to hide, she was under the microscope and felt damned certain that this bolshy, brave girl would get it out of her, come what may. She attempted to stem the flow of tears that were welling up inside her. Holly saw this coming, but had no patience for it.

"Don't bother turning on the waterworks. No-one out there has any sympathy for you and if you think I give a damn about your sudden rush of conscience, you can think again. How do you think all your victims felt whilst you were stamping on them and putting out cigarettes on their arms?" Nobody would be coming to save her. Fighting through tears and sobbing loudly as she spoke, Bella tried to explain as best she could. "I hate myself!" she roared with naked, primeval emotion.

I don't have a family. I never knew my father and my mother is a druggie. I was abused by my step-father between the ages of 8 and 12 before he was sent to prison."

"What, so I have to feel sorry for you now?" said Holly, incredulously. "You had a tough life so far. That's not unheard of. Many people would perhaps feel some sympathy for you...but you know what? That doesn't give you any special right to do what you've been doing to other people. Didn't it ever occur to you that it might have been better to treat people with respect? To be kind to them rather than bully them and browbeat them?"

"No-one ever showed me any kindness!" exclaimed Bella. Holly sprung up from her crouched position and laid down the law. "Don't you dare play the victim here! Take responsibility for your actions. You need to reflect on the pain you have caused others through no fault of their own. You and your stupid friends have simply gone out and preyed on people who you think are weaker than you....and for what?" Just so that you could feel better about yourself?"

Shaking her head in disgust, she looked briefly at her mobile and saw that a whole raft of comments was building steadily in the lower half of the screen. It seemed that everyone had an opinion on what was unfolding in this mysterious location. Someone had written the comment "it seems we have a vigilante in our midst." Seeing this gave Holly a momentary swell of pride.

"You need to take a good long look at yourself, Bella. My cousin will be OK, thank god, because he has a good family around him, no thanks to you. His cuts and bruises will heal, but as far his psychological scars, who can say? You and those other idiots have *no right* to go around acting like Hitler's brownshirts dishing out wanton violence to anyone you see fit. It stops now, do you hear me?" She raised her fist in anticipation of non-compliance but that ship had sailed and the message it seemed, had truly hit home.

Something in Bella's countenance had changed; it was as if she had reached a new level of understanding. "If it doesn't...so help me god. I mean it." Bella could see that Holly was deadly serious. "It will never happen again. You have my word. I'm truly sorry." Taking three slow and deliberate steps back toward the spot where she had left her rucksack perched at the base of a tree, Holly muttered a few final words under her breath, "here endeth the lesson."

Quickly removing the mini camera, tossing it into her bag and sliding her arms through it so that it sat tightly on her back once again, she skipped like a seasoned marine through the bushes and away into the night. Bella continued to lie on the floor for some time and had ample opportunity to digest the impact of what Holly had said to her. Eventually, in some discomfort, she dragged herself to her feet and limped home.

The next day was Saturday and to her surprise, she woke to some commotion in the house. Leaping out of bed and donning a dressing gown, she skipped down the stairs and encountered her mother at the kitchen table, preparing breakfast for them both. A wry smile played at the corners of her mouth. "Well, here she is - my vigilante daughter." "Huh?" was all Holly could offer in reply.

Her mother went on to explain that following the Facebook streaming event of yesterday afternoon, Holly had somehow overnight become something of a neighbourhood sensation after a local news station had got hold of the feed and deduced that this was a local girl fighting for justice in the face of ineffective leadership at the top of her school.

Consequently in the days that followed, the incumbent headteacher had offered his resignation and been replaced by a new, forward thinking headteacher who firmly believed in the values of kindness, benevolence and empathy.

The new head actively sought out the views of Holly, appointing her as an anti-bullying ambassador for the school, whilst Bella Mayfield was a changed person and went to great lengths to make amends for those she had previously harmed. Without their de facto leader to guide them, the wider gang of girls simply disbanded and had no choice but to correct their ways under the new and decisive leadership provided by the new headteacher.

For Holly it was an important victory, good had triumphed over evil, civility over anarchy and with this landmark achievement out of the way, she decided to set her sights on moving up to her next belt in karate. It wouldn't be long before this bravest of young woman would go on to clinch the coveted black belt. It would be a brave individual that would have dared to tangle with her.

TWILIGHT IN BARCELONA

Somewhere just off La Rambla in Barcelona on a sultry May evening, an American tourist sat outside a pavement cafe watching the world go by. In that most artistic and vibrant of all European cities, he felt truly at home.

It was the kind of place where you could simply lose yourself by wandering around its labyrinthine streets, casually observing all kinds of colourful street performers, opera singers, human statues and flamenco dancers.

To him, it was wonderfully intoxicating stuff and he considered the city to be the finest of all when it came to impromptu wandering. Naturally, the experience improved even further when you factored in the magnificent cuisine and fine wines.

He'd been sat there for just over an hour but didn't feel any great inclination to move on. People watching was ample entertainment. Characters from all walks of life milled past like a slow moving tide of flotsam and jetsam. A veritable roll call. There were happy-go-lucky teenagers, noisy and boisterous in their energetic exchanges, young lovers walking hand-in-hand, lost in each other's eyes, old fatigued couples, presumably long married, looking haggard and grumbling their way through recurrent quarrels as they trudged past.

The manifold melting pot of races and nationalities on display were remarkable, as were the varied languages he could hear. Since he'd first sat down in this spot, his ears had discerned a minimum of nine different tongues that he could confidently recognise, all of them with their own stories to tell and their own missions to carry out.

The tourist felt a sudden, inexplicable pang of sadness in his heart. He ruminated at length and determined that the cause of his regret was that of all the many people he witnessed passing by were merely doing just that - *passing through* - he would likely never see them again in his life. He took a tentative sip of the deeply coloured rioja which sat just in front of him. *All this criss-crossing of life on this busy, overcrowded planet of ours...What does it all mean? Is there any meaning to it at all?*

A waiter dressed in a crisp white shirt and pressed black trousers interrupted his reverie. "Are you fine, Señor?" Jerked away temporarily from his musings, the American gently lifted his palm. "I'm fine, *gracias*." With a courteous smile and a small bow, the waiter withdrew. Left once again to his own devices, he cast his eyes upward toward the ancient windows of the crumbling buildings that lined this narrow street.

What history they have packed into each and every crevice he considered. He felt as though he were inside a real life Gaudi painting and the sheer *joie de vivre* of Catalonian life washed over him like a soothing balm. He wondered inwardly whether he might find a way to stay here and not go back to his homeland. To remain in this city for good.

Smoothing his hand over his chin, any number of dreamlike scenarios began to play out in his mind's eye. These days, it's possible to work from anywhere, right? I could just become a *digital nomad*. A beautiful woman walked past and drew his attention away as she swept across his field of vision.

Looking longingly after her until she had disappeared out of sight, he shook his head wistfully and taking the wine glass in his hand, he swivelled it around, studying the rich purple hues of the chosen libation.

His peace wasn't to last long. Across to his right, two table lengths away, a particularly rowdy troupe of drunken men had noisily plonked themselves down and had begun obnoxiously clicking their fingers at the waiting staff, demanding a round of beers. Their belligerence sent ripples through what had previously been a pleasantly relaxed group of customers, hoping for nothing more than a quiet drink.

Considering it better to avoid eye contact with the new arrivals for fear of engaging in conversation and possibly, confrontation with them, he gulped down the wine, dug his hands into his pockets and pulled out a €20 note, strode up to the till and handed it cheerily enough to the somewhat flummoxed head waiter.

The apologetic look of contrition on the guy's face was perfectly self-explanatory. He couldn't exactly turn away passing trade, no matter how seemingly unsavoury the accompanying protagonists might be. Waving away the change he was due which was met with a grateful clasp of the hand, the American nodded his thanks for the hospitality bestowed upon him and rejoined the street theatre.

With no particular place to go, he ambled along aimlessly for a short while. Carrying a vague sense that he was in close proximity to the main thoroughfare of La Rambla, he scanned the walls of the buildings for a clue as to his location. He read the name of this street as **Carrer de la Portaferrissa**.

Twilight slowly gave way to nightfall, but the warmth remained and he began to feel somewhat sticky in a blue cotton shirt and white chinos. Thankfully, his choice of footwear was a functional and comfortable pair of kickers which softened his many steps.

Having no commitments or prior engagements to attend to, he was happy to wander freely, entirely of his own accord. The city was his to explore and he felt quite at home playing the role of a free spirit. There was a magical, unmistakable feeling of spring in the air - full of possibilities, fresh beginnings, hope and renewal. He felt it keenly in his breast and he wandered around with a broad grin on his face.

Some of the people he passed returned his smile, others looked at him as though he'd just burst into operatic song like a madman. None of this bothered him and so he carried on beaming like a Cheshire cat.

A quick check of his wristwatch told him that it was now 9.15pm. He started to feel faint pangs of hunger and stopped to examine the menu of an inviting looking restaurant. He had just finished working his way through the mouthwatering starters on offer when he felt a small tug at his right sleeve.

Looking down, he started at the sight of a young girl who he guessed, could not have been much more than 8 years old. She spoke to him in heavily accented, broken English. "Mister, I think you are being followed." He stared down at her, confusion spreading across his brow like ripples across a pond. *"What?"*

Instinctively, he patted his back pocket to ensure his wallet remained in place, feeling a little shameful in his cynicism, but being familiar with various apocryphal hard luck stories in his time of people who had been relieved of their wallets by cleverly orchestrated street choreography.

Keeping his hand on his wallet, he peered back up the street behind him, trying to make sense of this unexpected notice, but in the vast, moving crowd he could not see anyone that conformed to the pattern of the mysterious young girl's forewarning.

He decided to adopt a change of tone. "Look, young lady. I don't know exactly what your game is here, but I don't see anyone coming after me and I've no reason to believe that I have made any enemies." Her eyes seemed to glaze over and it was apparent that she had not really understood his words. He tried again.

Speaking more slowly, using a plainer choice of vocabulary, he decided to introduce a series of sweeping gestures to his speech. Pointing to his chest, he began. "Me - friends with *everybody*." At this, he spread his arms far and wide to indicate a unanimous verdict. "No have problem. No *want* problem!" He grimaced at his own clumsy effort at 'dumbed down English for Spanish street children' and felt at a loss as to what he should do.

Just then, a harangued-looking, follically challenged older man wearing a dark suit burst out of the restaurant and started remonstrating with the young girl whilst casting humbly apologetic looks toward the tourist.

Once the initial confusion of this escalation had started to wear off, he realised what had taken place. The guy had clearly noted the young girl down as a panhandler or hustler of some kind and simultaneously eyeing the tourist up as a potential customer, sought to extricate him by dispersing the child and offering him shelter at one of the cosy looking tables inside his candle lit restaurant.

The kerfuffle left the tourist in a kind of daze and he was rendered nothing more than a statue until roused from his daydream by the waiter who was gesturing that he should follow him inside where he possessed the various riches of an ample supply of wine, tapas and live music.

Although he obediently followed the exuberant restaurateur into his establishment, he couldn't help but feel a sense of wrongdoing toward the girl who remained at a safe distance across the square, her expressionless eyes fixed on him. Whenever he turned around to look back, he could see her looking directly at him. It was unsettling and caused him to lose his appetite entirely.

Irrational panic struck him. *What if she is some kind of gypsy? Could she put a curse on me?"* The food - assorted plates of tapas which he had not personally chosen but which regardless came automatically - arrived, and delicious though they looked, he had by that time decidedly lost his appetite. The owner, who was of the attentive variety, came over to his table and asked the tourist if everything was alright.

He offered weakly that he'd eaten a large meal earlier, but would of course be happy to pay for the food they had so kindly provided. The owner simply nodded in a neutral fashion and gathered up the plates. All was silent in the restaurant for a good ten minutes.

The tourist next raised his hand and asked for the bill, noting the time. It was now 10.35pm. Most Spanish families it seemed, were just getting down to the main course. He peeked out from the alcove where he was sitting behind a thick wall and noted with a sudden shock that the young girl was still standing across the square and looking in his direction.

He felt utterly unsettled and decided to ask the owner if there was a different exit, perhaps at the rear of the restaurant? For the first time that night, the owner's previous friendly nature deserted him; with a derisory look, he simply exclaimed "you are scared of little girls, que no?" The tourist bridled at this suggestion and went red in the face. "Do you have one or not?" he demanded, suddenly rattled. "Not. Only the front entrance."

Throwing his hands up in exasperation at this foreigner's strange behaviour, the owner stomped off to his kitchen, leaving the tourist to face his young antagonist who waited patiently for him to leave the establishment.

He decided that the whole thing was ridiculous and after leaving payment for his uneaten meal atop his table, he strode purposefully across the square to where the young girl stood, statuesque. Her expression barely altered as he approached her. "You wait for me a long time," he said matter-of-factly. "I tell you already, mister. Somebody follow you. I don't know why they follow," she retorted.

He looked at her, studying her face for some moments and eventually let out a long, drawn-out sigh. "Where are your parents?" She shot straight back at him without emotion. "I have no parents. Is just me." He blinked a few times and ran his hand through his hair as if to cope with this shocking announcement.

The girl simply remained impassive. "Where are you staying?" I sleep in *La Sagrada Familia*," declared the girl. "The basilica?" spluttered the tourist. Taking a moment to digest this declaration, he withheld the many questions that formed a lengthy queue in his mind.

After some time, he spoke up. "Can you show me?" enquired the tourist. The young girl simply nodded. "It will take 30 minutes to walk," she offered, casting a doubtful look over the tourist as though she imagined a taxi would be far preferable to his tastes. In the event, he was happy to walk and together with this most atypical of tour guides, the strange couple made their way across the buzzing city - which was only just coming to life - before they arrived at the gothic masterpiece whose construction had begun in 1882 and was infamous for still not being finished.

The word was that completion was expected in time for the centenary of Gaudi's death in 2026. The young girl had indeed spoken the truth; she led the American to a somewhat surprising sight - that of a modern day commune, hidden in plain sight and yet living in the grounds of the giant building.

Facilities were not much better than those of the average homeless person. Resources were scarce, but they had sleeping bags, shared resources and appeared to be united by a deep faith in God. The tourist was humbled by what he saw and felt a renewed shame for how he had initially perceived the child.

He had not expected to see something like this, that was for sure. A lump formed in his throat. "You really stay here?" he stammered, incredulous. She simply nodded and swept a young arm over the scene that lay before them. "These all my friends. We are like big family."

Somewhere a clock struck midnight and a strong wave of sleepiness came over the tourist. Wordlessly, he clasped a €100 note into the small hands of the tough young heroine before stealing away into the shadows of the night, hurriedly flagging down a taxi, heading back to his rented apartment and his comparatively privileged life.

Naturally, he felt rather cowardly at slinking away but if he was truly honest with himself, he just didn't want to have to deal with such problems. Truth be told, he'd been running away from tough situations his whole life.

Safely ensconced back in his bed that night, he found himself reflecting on the lessons of the evening. He considered anew the mysteries of life, how some people are born seemingly into great hardship, others into great advantage and the rest of them somewhere in the middle.

He knew it was unlikely that he'd ever see that remarkable young lady again, but he felt glad to have met her and would never forget his experience of witnessing with his own eyes that strange place she called home.

THE AGE OF UNREASON

The stage was set. Make-up artists were applying the final flourishes to the rather smug and self-satisfied TV presenter who it was widely suspected, was more interested in how he looked and was perceived by his viewers than the content of the debate which was taking place in front of him.

Entitled (not entirely without a trace of irony) *Hot Potato,* his weekly show brought together two 'marmite' figures who stood unashamedly for their particular cause or argument and whom frequently represented the most bullish and dogmatic of figures, all of which was quite naturally designed to generate the maximum controversy and by extension, drive up viewing figures.

Preening like a peacock, shifting the angle of his gaze and pausing to adjust his tie, he enquired of the female make-up artist who stood in front of him how he looked. The lady knew by now that it was simply easier to massage the guy's ego. "Splendid, darling!" came the rather self-congratulatory response.

The two figures located either side of him were in somewhat less relaxed mood and shifted edgily in their respective chairs. They were both highly respected debaters, well educated and held in high esteem by the divided camps for which they put forward their case. It could not be said by any stretch of the imagination however, that they were neutrally minded, let alone easy to get on with.

They had almost made it their political capital to provoke, to kindle flames and to set tongues wagging. The topic of this particular debate was centered around the rise of *wokism* and the renewed efforts of feminists and black lives matter campaigners to draw attention to their causes.

Representing the left leaning viewpoint was a Guardian columnist named Xavier Roberts-Smith and speaking on behalf of the right-leaning audience was an established author of books on political theory and independent blogger named Jasmine Teller.

The studio audience waited with baited breath for this hotly anticipated clash of ideologies to begin, feeling certain that sparks would fly. It was no great secret that these two individuals had little time for one another - indeed, they had clashed - verbally at any rate - in highly publicised spats on a number of previous occasions.

Clearing his throat loudly and proceeding to push his glasses up to the bridge of his nose with showy pretentiousness, the presenter waited for the countdown that was delivered via the hand signals of the floor manager to reach zero before launching into his spiel, smooth as silk. He spoke with a rich, syrup-like voice.

"Good evening. On tonight's show, we welcome to the panel Xavier Roberts-Smith and Jasmine Teller to the panel to discuss one of the weightier issues of our times - at this point, he paused, dramatically - the modern phenomenon of "woke," a term which refers to a perceived awareness of social and racial justice. It is said to derive from the African-American vernacular, to "*stay woke.*" He looked around the audience over the tip of his glasses in the manner of a stern academic ensuring he has the full attention of his students.

The presenter went on. "Now, this is a particularly emotive issue and one which has increasingly gained in prominence over the last few years, halted by neither Brexit nor Covid-19. High profile incidents of police brutality and alleged systematic discrimination in everyday society..." he was cut off at this point with a derisive snort from the Guardian columnist.

Looking questioningly at him, Xavier countered with a retort. "It's hardly alleged, now is it? The United Kingdom is one of the most racist countries in the world, for heaven's sake!" "Utterly ludicrous..." came the sharp reply. Before anyone had even settled in their seats, they were off. Two verbal gladiators slugging it out, each of them determined to put forward their diametrically opposed point of view, no matter what.

"Now hold on," began the presenter, trying to restore a semblance of order. "You'll both have ample opportunity to have your say." Like naughty school children, the two guests leaned back in their chair sulkily and whistled under their breath, positively bursting to score points.

Noticing with relief that someone had helpfully paused the autocue for him, he now turned back to it and resumed his preamble. "With the UK and indeed the rest of the world so divided on the various issues, we are today asking the fundamental question: "*What is the end goal here?*" Where do the leaders of Black Lives Matters want to get to? For feminist leaders, "how far are you willing to go in order to achieve your stated goals of equality?" A few members of the audience shifted uncomfortably in their seats.

Turning to the political theorist, he kicked things off. "Jasmine, you're regarded as a representative of the centre-right, conservative in values and outlook - some might say, a *traditionalist*." There was a small outbreak of tittering in the audience at this.

The 33 year old author who was of mixed race, certainly didn't look like the archetypal home-counties blue rinse Tory voter. If anything, when looking at her counterpart Xavier, the untrained eye might reasonably have assumed that their loyalties lay in the opposing camps. He was 29 years old, Oxford educated, white, privileged. The only difference being that he spoke with a deliberately earthy, Northern accent and made great capital out of having relatives who lived in the mill towns of Lancashire. Jasmine spoke with a firmly middle-class London media-centric accent.

"How do you view these issues and what are your thoughts on our general direction of travel?" concluded the didactic host. Jasmine didn't pause for thought, opting instead to launch straight into her narrative. "We have a real problem in this country," she began, her face reflecting a most earnest expression. "We are witnessing what I call *the rise of liberal facism*.

Political correctness has gone beyond a joke, the freedom of speech is being threatened like never before and frankly, the lunatics have taken over the running of the asylum." A brief smattering of applause followed this as her opponent sitting opposite, shook his head with withering contempt. Jasmine continued. "Statues are being torn down, mob rule is apparently being given credibility over the rule of law.

These people - at this she pointed an angry finger in the direction of Xavier - seemingly wish to rewrite history, starting with the colonial history of this great country of ours!" The man from the Guardian couldn't help himself. "We do have a problem in this country - people like *you!*" A separate section of the audience then offered their vocal reinforcement of this charge and the presenter, testily raised an arm, exclaiming "Thank you Xavier, you'll have your say in due course." This split the audience with some offering fervent approval for this apparently impartial shutdown, whilst those in the other camp demanded redress, immediately if not sooner.

The presenter looked expectantly at Jasmine to continue with her answers. "It has been the case for some time now that the *loony left* as I like to refer to them have been shouting louder and louder for what they perceive as the rights of the underdog, the trampled, the great unwashed..." She lent an exaggerated dramatism to these terms, almost mockingly in the direction of Xavier.

"How many times have we read about real life examples where the human rights of a criminal, a terrorist of a paedophile have taken precedent over the victim?" She got another round of applause for this statement. "I mean, I don't know about you in the audience, but I'm getting to the point where I can't bear to visit the BBC News website anymore.

Every single story and article continually force-feeds us the narrative of the aforementioned 'downtrodden' without realising that by pushing their great creed of so called "equality and inclusivity," that they are actually deeply guilty of *positive discrimination*. Driven purely by, I hasten to add - white middle class guilt."

This was simply too much for Xavier, who by this point looked crimson with righteous indignation. "Utter nonsense! Typical right-wing extremism, spouted by someone who should know better," he said with barbed accusation in his voice. She shot back instantly. "Someone who should know better?" she demanded. Sparks were really starting to fly now. The presenter thought briefly about trying to restore order, but the prospect of soaring ratings overrode his judgement.

"Could it possibly be, Xavier that you aren't just falling into the very trap I've just highlighted? She stared at him, her eyes flashing daggers. "What on earth are you talking about?" he asked, with more than a hint of trepidation in his countenance. "You think that as a mixed-race female who grew up in South London, I should automatically bang the drum for the liberal elite - is that it?

Xavier seemed to realise that he'd wandered into a trap and cursed under his breath. "That's the last thing I would assume, as you very well know. I believe in a cause which does *not* judge a book by its' cover." "Unless they're of the Jewish persuasion, perhaps?" said Jasmine, cynically.

There was a palpable, simmering tension growing in the studio and the presenter saw this as his chance to interject. "You are referring, I assume to the former leader of the Labour party's alleged antisemitism..? he ventured. "Accusations which were unreliable at best and have now been comprehensively addressed," insisted Xavier.

"They were hardly unreliable," replied Jasmine, addressing her remark directly to the audience with a conspiratorial look. "I lost count of how many MPs resigned in protest at the matter," she added nonchalantly. "There's no smoke without fire, Xavier." She felt as though she had him exactly where she wanted. He was rattled and had apparently lost that first crucial point which undermined his credibility significantly.

"Yes, I think we might be drifting slightly from the point," said the presenter, fluidly. "The second question if you recall, was around the direction of travel." Jasmine drew a brief intake of breath, as though she was summoning the right words with which to make her argument. "I actually believe that we are headed in a worrying direction."

She trained her eyes on the camera which was pointed directly at her and held a grave expression. "We have authors, comedians, poets and scriptwriters telling us that they are literally frightened for younger artists coming through and trying to make a name for themselves. Why? This is thanks to another phenomenon created by the left. It's called *cancel culture,* folks and it is spreading like a disease. Forget Coronavirus - this poisonous ideology is spreading much faster."

There were some groans at this comparison across the audience, in some cases, outright anger. She went on. "Imagine some of our oldest national treasures who have enjoyed long, successful careers of 30, maybe 40 years. Imagine how hard they worked to get where they are, think about their achievements and the impact for good they have had on the world. Then imagine that they've committed the mortal sin of speaking out on a topic which they don't necessarily agree with, feel comfortable about or worse yet, is not in line with the ideology of the liberal elite.

Then what happens? A robust, healthy debate which sits in line with our deepest traditions of free speech and open discussion? Not a bit of it. They are roundly shamed, humiliated, made to feel that they've committed some kind of atrocity and their careers which they worked so far, effectively cancelled. Is this fair? Is this right?

Further ripples of applause accompanied her rising passion, louder than before. Xavier began to shout across her. "How much more of this right-wing ranting must we endure...?" Jasmine raised her hand, firmly. "Xavier. Let me finish, please. You'll have your say in a moment."

The audience chuckled as one, recognising the near non-existent role of the presenter, so used to preening in front of the cameras. Today, he was getting far less airtime than usual. "I'll finish my point by saying that whilst lessons should and could be learned from the more shameful chapters in our history, we should never make the mistake of trying to somehow re-write history or pretend that certain things never took place.

This is an extremely dangerous way of thinking. It's rather like those imbeciles down in Bristol who thought it was acceptable to vandalise a statue that was built to commemorate someone who died 300 years ago - as though anyone can actually apply the standards and behaviour of the early 18th century to Britain in 2021.

Do these people really believe that we should all pay the price for what took place ten or eleven generations ago? Such thinking just goes to show the irrationality of these people and their extremely dangerous beliefs. I'd like to finish if I may by sharing the following famous Oscar Wilde quote:- *"I may not agree with you, but I will defend to the death your right to make an ass of yourself."*

At the conclusion of this, precisely half of the audience broke out in confirmatory applause whilst the others looked as though they wanted to storm the stage there and then. The presentator, seeing his opportunity to quickly jump in and seize the initiative back from his loquacious panellist, did so. "Thank you, Jasmine. I'd now like to pose the same two questions to Xavier."

The man from the Guardian waited impatiently for the applause to subside, looking rather like a champagne bottle that had been shaken up and needed to be uncorked. He spoke with a tone of disapproving indignation. "Well, thank you Jasmine for taking the trouble to *almost* mention the rather crucial issue of slavery. A true stain if ever there was one, on our collective national conscience."

Jasmine couldn't help adding another riposte. "What they never tell you of course is that it was the African princes who sold their own people to the colonialists, but never mind *that* inconvenient truth, eh Xavier?" This really enraged him and he thumped the desk sharply with a flat palm.

"Will you be quiet?!" he demanded of her. "Oh dear. Telling a woman to be quiet live on TV. If our allegiances were the other way around, what would be the chances of *me* being a victim of 'cancel culture?'

The presentator saw at once that he would have to restore order. "Now, both of you listen to me please. There are certain rules that we must abide by. I appreciate that you both hold your respective positions and speak with passion for your cause, but I must insist that we follow the guidelines here."

He paused, again in the manner of a schoolmaster admonishing two unruly pupils. A look of contrition from Jasmine reassured him sufficiently to hand the floor back over to Xavier. It was his turn to speak.

"Thank you. I think every right minded person in this country believes in creating a better and fairer world which gives each and every one of its citizens equality of opportunity. A country which doesn't discriminate based on the colour of a person's skin, their religious beliefs nor their starting position in life.

Which is why I for one, will not stop fighting until the board of every FTSE 250 company has at least equal female representation, each religious group is represented in their town or village by a place of worship, whether that be a mosque, a temple or a synagogue.

Women should be paid the same as men, if not more! I also believe there should be a reparation fund set up, similar to that of foreign aid for those who suffered at the hands of slavery thanks to our colonial ancestors. This is the 21st century, and so traditional systems and structures that oppress and enslave should be completely done away with.

Growing unrest in the audience again highlighted the division of backers and opponents. Xavier went on. "Our moves to recognise gender neutrality and equal rights for transgender individuals must be continued and where necessary, people re-educated on such matters." "Wow…" came the stunned response from Jasmine who had refrained from comments until now.

"The sheer *arrogance* of your position, not to mention the insanity of it all. Do you honestly believe…" at this, Xavier began to shout back at her and their raised voices combined to create an almighty din, impenetrable to anyone but themselves.

The presenter raised his hand to his ear, not to block out the noise and clamour, but to hear the message that was being relayed to him via his earpiece. The colour drained from his face and he suddenly leapt out of his chair with spectacular urgency.

"Bomb! There's a bomb in the studio! Everybody out…" The room transformed into a chaotic blur of panicked individuals, all scurrying for the exits, pushing and shoving, in some cases trampling over each other in their desperation.

As a result, this intensive debate, so indicative of our times, was never finished and no consensus reached. It was ever thus…

IN THE GLORIOUS MONTH OF MAY

Lush, fragrant banks of wild bluebells fanned out around him as he trudged contentedly through the early May woods. There wasn't another soul in sight, nor in earshot as he reflected with happy solitude upon the heart-warming beauty of the archetypal Cotswold scene all around him.

Birds chirped and the occasional furtive rabbit darted nervously from one side of the path to the other, all of which seemed to be in perfect keeping with the rhythm and the cadence of the forest.

An older man approaching his winter years, he had always carried the mantra "no regrets" and believed firmly in looking forward, never backward. Widowed for almost 7 years, he had loved and lost his childhood sweetheart and there wasn't a single day that passed in which he didn't think about her radiant smile, her light and cheerful countenance.

He shivered as a wave of sadness seemed to shudder right through to his very core. A blue tit sang its familiar song as rays of sunlight dappled through the treetops. He had been walking for just over 2 hours at a steady pace and beads of sweat had started to form unsightly rings around his collar and under his armpits.

Shedding his jacket, he paused to stuff it into his already crammed rucksack. Surveying the immaculately peaceful scene in front of him, he gazed in all directions around him. A squirrel remained frozen, mid-motion with furtive eyes locked upon him uneasily, as if waiting for him to commit to his next move.

Despite the familiar aches and pains involved in doing so, the old man slowly crouched down and remained on his haunches, keeping his eyes on his bushy-tailed friend, taking great care not to give the small creature to be startled. Abruptly, it darted off out of sight and the old man, with a small groan hauled himself back to his feet.

He'd been just 7 years old when he'd first laid eyes on the girl. They had moved all the way from Scotland down to the West Country on account of his Father's post in the Royal Air Force. It was a seismic change from what they had been used to before.

He'd effectively had to start again, to make a whole collection of new friends, to get used to a new set of teachers and different surroundings. He particularly remembered being singled out at his school for *sounding* different.

The gentle, lilting tones of his Edinburgh accent must have contrasted sharply with the bucolic burr he now encountered. The light hearted ribbing didn't last long, however and he soon settled into his new life and made firm friends with his new classmates.

His little sister, who was 3 years younger than him and who now lived in faraway New Zealand was a great comfort to him and undoubtedly he to her.

They used to whisper to each other through the thin walls of their new home at night and stuck together through what was initially at least, a tumultuous time. He stopped pensively to think about his sister, so far away from him and yet in this miraculous modern world of technology and gadgetry, not really at that far.

After all, it was ridiculously easy to merely press a few buttons and see her face on a computer screen, despite her being the best part of 12,000 miles away. The mundanity of discussing the weather, grandchildren and growing old seemed somehow ironic when you considered the lofty achievement that was internet based video calling.

He mused back to the way Pathé newsreel announcers used to speak, their enunciation and even how they wore evening dress to simply read the news. Chuckling to himself, he remembered that he was actually out in the open and that anyone who happened to be observing him at that precise moment might reasonably assume that there was something not quite right about him.

Taking a moment to glance at this watch, he trudged on. It was an exceptionally beautiful time of year to be in England. There was a palpable freshness in the air, everything seemed to be bursting with fragrance, green shouts abounded and pretty flowers of all shades and colours bobbed gently in the soft wind.

Nature was his tonic, there was no question about that. If he should feel at any time stressed, morose, anxious, all he had to do was head into the great outdoors and he would find salvation.

He didn't particularly care for the endless greyness and rain that seems to hold the country in its foreboding grip from the back end of autumn, right through the first signs of life in late March, but he could cope nonetheless with all seasons and whatever they threw at him.

Over the course of several years, he and his childhood sweetheart had been on innumerable walking holidays and along the way had built up a staggering collection of ordnance survey maps, which charted every square inch of these isles with remarkable attention to detail.

Together, they had derived so much pleasure from using these worn and weathered documents as they explored thousands of paths, bridleways, beaches and woods. His heart panged at the deep expanse of all those cherished memories.

Switching his attention somewhat forcibly back to the immediate task at hand, he considered the remaining distance of his planned route. As a traditionalist who took the purist's approach when it came to cartographic matters, he eschewed the modern penchant for pedometers and mobile mapping apps, like a crusty old sailor who stubbornly retains his compass in place of GPS.

By his reckoning, he would arrive back at his car in approximately 90 minutes. His estimate was that he had around 5 miles to go and since he walked relatively quickly (at a pace between 3 and 4 mph,) that should leave ample time to stop for a brief rest along the way.

There seemed to be nobody around - in fact, he hadn't seen another soul for at least 20 minutes which was perhaps a little strange. All of a sudden and to his considerable discomfort, he heard a distant cry of some sort. It sounded like a woman's voice, but he couldn't be sure that it hadn't been a child calling out.

The sounds appeared to be coming from somewhere up ahead. He didn't need to glance at this map - he knew the area well enough to be able to trace all of its paths and bridleways on the back of his hand. He deduced that the sound must be coming from a narrow path leading along the edge of an ancient woodland up ahead to the right. He suspected that a fellow walker might be in trouble and resolved to investigate and do what he could to assist. Adding to his gait a swift nimbleness that belied his advanced years, he started in the direction of where the sound had come from.

Before long, he heard another call for help and knew for sure that he was on the correct path. This time it seemed clear that it was a woman's voice - plainative, somewhat panicked, perhaps that of an older woman? Placing his cupped hands either side of his mouth by way of amplification, he bellowed a reply.

"Don't worry, help is on the way. I'll be right with you!" He didn't quite know what the correct protocol was in such a situation and was effectively ad-libbing. Regardless, somebody was in trouble and he felt obliged to try and help the stricken individual.

The path he now followed was decidedly narrow and closely hugged the edge of a crop field on one side and an ancient wood on the other. As it was, there was little room for one and he fervently hoped that he wouldn't meet someone coming the other way.

An electrified fence straddling the tapered path complicated matters further and he had to be careful not to reach out for balance and accidently grab the metal rail since he had no way of knowing whether or not it was actually live.

Rounding a corner, he happened upon the source of those anxious cries. He stopped dead in his tracks. A 70-something lady, appropriately dressed for the occasion in walking garb, boots and stuffed rucksack was caught in an inadvertent trap, her waterproof jacket having become attached to the electric fence, rendering her unable to risk disentangling herself without the very real risk of getting an electric shock. Like an upturned turtle, she was unable to right herself and was pretty helpless.

It was an altogether different type of shock which had stopped the old man in his tracks, however. The detained lady who appeared right in front of him, looked the spitting image of his former wife. It was almost uncanny and completely unsettled the old man. The relief on the lady's face was tangible. "Oh thank goodness. I'm so sorry to trouble you like this, but I appear to be in something of a pickle and cannot wriggle free for some reason."

Regaining his ruffled composure at length, he replied. "Your waterproof is entangled with the electric fence," explained the old man, helpfully. "Here, let me see if I can't help set you free." He approached the old lady cautiously, aware not only of the danger presented by the fence, but of the social awkwardness posed by the meeting of two strangers in such an unusual situation.

Gingerly, he worked with practised hands and gradually loosened the twisted straps of her jacket, freeing her from her rather odd prison. "There we are. Right as rain now!" A proud man who some-times came across a rather stiff and off-hand to those who didn't know him intimately, he felt somewhat bashful and tongue-tied in the company of other women and this situation was no differ-ent. To his relief, she laughed off her misadventure and proved to be a thoroughly affable and charming lady.

"Which way are you heading?" she enquired of him. "Back to my car at….let me see now, Braddock Wood." "Braddock Wood?" she replied, thoughtfully. "There's a nice little tearoom over there, adjacent to the car park if I recall correctly."

She looked him squarely in the eyes, with an ever so slightly mis-chievous gleam that spoke of a light-hearted free spirit. "Well…" he began, somewhat diffident. "At least allow me to buy you a cup of tea as thanks for coming along. I might have been stuck there all night, god forbid!"

The two silver-haired companions got along instantly and en-joyed a very pleasant amble which took them after what didn't feel like long to the tearoom in question.

Over afternoon tea, the old man learned that his new friend was in fact a widow and in turn, he told her that he himself was a widower. Call it serendipity, call it sheer coincidence - whatever it was, the two of them seemed made for each other, giving rise to the very real possibility of a wonderful new companionship.

A CHILD'S FANTASY

The little girl burst into her mother's bedroom, gripped with excitement. "Mummy, Mummy! I had the weirdest dream *ever!*" The child's mother groaned softly as she was forcibly roused from a deep slumber of her own, registering through blurry, scrunched up eyes courtesy of her mobile phone that it was only 6.43am on Saturday morning.

"Isabelle, sweetheart. It's not time to get up yet. Remember when we spoke about this," pleaded her mother, her speech interspersed with stifled yawns. The little girl was excitable however and persisted. "But Mummy! My memory has been stolen and I've only got 59 minutes to get it back!" The mother stared at her daughter, askance. "Huh?" was about all she could muster to this unexpected proclamation.

"I'm version 7.52-ZQJB," stated Isabelle, matter of factly. Now her mother sat up and squinted at the insistent little girl. *Was this some sci-fi type game that she was meant to know about? Was she missing a trick here?* "Sweetheart, it's.." "58 minutes now, Mummy. You've *got* to help me." Caught somewhere between exasperation and genuine concern for this weird turn of events, she tried a calm approach with her daughter in the hope of making sense of it all. "Where is this all coming from, Izzy? Have you been watching a scary movie that you shouldn't have?"

The little girl shook her head decisively. "No. I just need you to help me find the password to get my memory back." Now her mother was even more confused. She simply studied the little girl, mouth agape. Isabelle went on, unfettered. "This is just a temporary file. When it deletes itself, I will have my memory wiped! Her mother searched her blunted mental repository for words, any words. "Are you feeling alright, my love?" She reached out to place a caring hand on young Isabelle's head to check for signs of a temperature.

"I feel totally fine, Mummy. I just need you to help me before it's too late!" Utterly bamboozled, her mother felt that she had little choice but to go along with whatever game her daughter was playing. It was just the two of them in this little house and had been for the past 18 months after Isabelle's father had walked out of their lives without warning.

Her mother felt that strong sense of guilt that all mothers feel when worrying about their children. Was this strange behaviour that her daughter now exhibited a direct result of all that chaos which had resulted from her Father's unexpected departure? Perhaps this was a coping mechanism of some sort, manifested into some kind of fantasy world. She just couldn't work it out.

Isabelle tugged at the duvet. "Come on, Mummy. We have to go find the password. I don't want to lose my memory!" It was genuine concern for her child's sanity that induced her to swing her legs out of the bed, pull on her slippers and don a dressing gown to accompany Isabelle across the landing and down the stairs.

Taking her mother by the hand, Isabelle hurriedly led her down into the living room where in the corner of the room on a small work desk sat an HP laptop. Janet, Isabelle's mother used it for her work but she never had a problem in allowing Isabelle to use it albeit under close supervision for the purposes of learning or leisure. Janet didn't want to be the type of parent who said no to something as important and pervasive as the internet.

She couldn't countenance the idea of other children in Isabelle's class having conversations about a learning game they'd played or a movie they might have watched which her daughter wasn't given access to. In her mind, it was about give and take, carefully overseeing things from a distance, but granting just enough freedom for her to remain part of the conversation and to have access to the right resources for her development.

"Can we go on Google, please Mummy?" begged Isabelle. "Yes, sweetheart." Janet looked on as the 6 year old nonchalantly typed a question into the Google search bar. *How can I retrieve my memory?* Janet's eyebrows raised at this. "Retrieved? That's quite a big word for a 6-year-old. How did you know about that?" she enquired. "The man in the dream told me," replied Isabelle, candidly. Janet grew concerned at this.

"The man in the dream?" she demanded with sudden urgency. "Yes. He was tall, with salt & pepper coloured hair, wore a suit and had bright green eyes," replied Isabelle. All of Janet's protectively motherly instincts went into overdrive. She reached out her arm and snapped the laptop shut with a bang. "Mummy?!"

Janet's tone sharpened and she fixed her daughter with a serious gaze. "I want you to tell Mummy exactly what is going on. What man? When? Did someone get into your room?" Little Isabelle simply shook her head. "No, silly. The man from the story you read to me last week."

None of this was making a great deal of sense to the jaded mental faculties of Janet. She took a moment to collect herself. "What do you need to search Google for?" The little girl replied perfectly calmly. "The man said that when the dream is finished, I will wake up and that I need to search for answers to retrieve my memory. He said that I will only have 60 minutes. If someone doesn't know the answer to a question, they have to Google it. Everyone does it,

Mummy!"

Janet smiled in spite of herself, full of admiration for her preco-
cious daughter's wordly-wise nature. How right she was. Indeed,
what did we all do prior to the existence of Google? Consult
encyclopedias, she supposed. Feeling a tinge of remorse for her
sharp rebuke and the manner in which she had sought to exert
control by slamming the laptop shut, Janet softened her stance
and decided that she would humour Isabelle's imagination after
all. Who knows, it might be fun?

Re-opening the laptop once again, they both embarked on a
voyage of discovery around the world wide web in the hope
of answering the impossibly vague question:- *How can I retrieve
my memory?* Predictably, all sorts of results appeared, span-
ning psychological theory, academic papers published by leading
neuroscientists and endless self-help guidance.

None of it seemed particularly enlightening in their somewhat
unique quest. "Mummy, it's 7.17am! That means I only have until
7.42am to find the password. We need to find it!" Janet couldn't
tell whether her little girl was being utterly serious or whether it
was part of the performance. Either way, she didn't truly believe
that there was actually any risk of her daughter's memory suddenly fragmenting at the appointed hour.

Time continued its inexorable march and it felt as though Janet
was going to have to come up with something special. There were
just five minutes left. Isabelle appeared to have become a little
distracted, having gravitated toward websites that showcased re-
views of well known toy brands. She certainly didn't exhibit any
strong signs of fearing her impending doom. Janet had to act and
fast. "I've got it!" she said, leaping up in a show of exaggerated triumph. "I know how to crack the code!" She had successfully cap-
tured Isabelle's attention, it was clear. The little girl turned her
gaze from that of the hypnotic screen to the heroic figure of her

mother.

"Isabelle. How many letters are there in our alphabet?" Isabelle's eyes lit up. "That's easy, Mummy. 26!" Janet beamed. "Yes, exactly! Now....let's say that each letter is equal to a number. For example, A=1, B=2, C=3 and so on..." Isabelle nodded her understanding, rapt. Now, can you spell out your full name for me?

Grinning widely, she took great pride in enunciating her name in the way that only a 6-year-old can. "Isabelle Amelia Simpson." Grabbing a pen and paper, Janet smiled right back at her and continued to explain. "Perfect. Now, we just need to convert each letter to the right number."

It took them both a few minutes to first sketch out a list, followed by the numbers. "Eureka! This is the password! 9-19-1-2-5-12-12-5 > 1-13-5-12-9-1 > 19-9-13-16-19-15-14. Let's say it out loud together." They did so and Janet clapped her hands together for dramatic effect. "Now, sweetheart. How old are you?" "6."

"Where do you live?" "Milton Keynes." "What is the name of your BFF?" "Sophie of course!" Janet looked at Isabelle expectantly, waiting for the penny to drop. The little girl's expression burst once more into unbridled joy and she flung her arms around her mother's neck, planting numerous scattered, affectionate kisses.

"You're the best Mummy ever!"

THE END

Printed in Great Britain
by Amazon